LAVENDER

b
michell

Kiki
and the Lost
Leprechaun

Published by Lavender Health Ltd.

A special thanks to my three children for their help in bringing this book to life, Paul who always believes in me and Mary, my mum. Also to my editor, Sandra Stafford and my illustrator Zoe Mellors for their patience and professionalism.

Lastly, thank you to my cousin Juliet Knight (www.julietknight.co.uk) for designing the cover and putting my book together.

The Lavender Maze Series
Kiki and the Lost Leprechaun

Author's foreword

As a child I loved reading books. I would lose myself for hours snuggled on the sofa reading, and I honestly have the happiest childhood memories of doing this. Even all those years ago, I dreamed of writing books for other children – and here it is: Kiki and the Lost Leprechaun. Some of you may prefer to hear this book read aloud by an adult. And some of you may prefer to read it alone. Whichever you choose, I hope you all enjoy this story of magic and mystery. And perhaps one day you will write a book too.

A note for adults

My Lavender Maze series, including Kiki and the Lost Leprechaun, is for a broad age range. I understand the importance of enjoying the story and also of improving vocabulary at the same time. Extended vocabulary words in this book have been emboldened, with a simple glossary after the final chapter. The glossary aims to increase readers' knowledge, actively engage them in the text, and help them to have a better, clearer understanding of these words.

"If you want your children to be intelligent, read them fairy tales. If you want them to be more intelligent, read them more fairy tales."

Albert Einstein

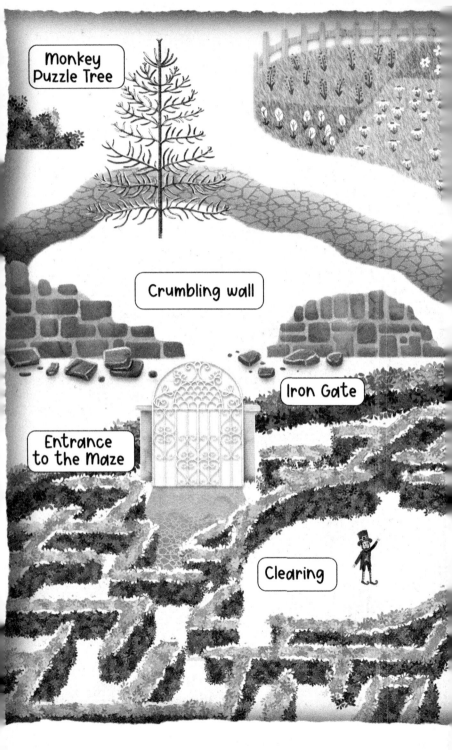

Cravendale Cottage

Nanny's
House

Wishy

Queenie

Bridge

Mermaid Lagoon

Chapter 1

"Good morning Nanny Stick," **beamed** Kiki as she skipped into Nanny Stick's kitchen.

The sun **glistened** through the **sash** window and **reflected** on Kiki's light brown hair, tied back in a red polka dot ribbon. "What is for breakfast? I'm

1

starving," she said with a cheeky grin. Nanny Stick giggled and pointed to the pot of cold porridge on the side. Nanny Stick loved cold porridge. Kiki didn't, and politely **declined**! "I think I'll pass on breakfast this morning," she said, **despite** being **ravenous**.

Kiki visited Nanny Stick every morning before school. Her Nanny lived in a small **annexe** attached to Cravendale Cottage. Well, it wasn't *exactly* a cottage. It was a large **picturesque** house surrounded by fields, similar to something you might see on a postcard. There were no other houses for miles around, and no noisy car engines or rumbling buses. Instead, were the faint neighs of horses grazing in nearby fields and the mooing of the cows feasting on the grassy hills.

Cravendale Cottage had been in Kiki's family for many **generations**. It had been the childhood home of Nanny Stick, where she grew up and where her mother also grew up. It was a magical house full of happy memories. The bricks were faded into a brownish-yellow colour, but there were always flowers growing around the house regardless of the season. There were daffodils and tulips in spring, tall sunflowers in summer and beautifully **scented** butterfly **ranunculi** in autumn. Then there were the snowdrops, which always lit up the winter sky. Whatever the season, Cravendale Cottage always looked **majestic**, and it was truly a special place to live.

The main front door was painted a light shade of violet. Next to it was another front door the same colour, but which had a sign above it reading: "Nanny's House". Nanny had her own entrance, her own bathroom, her own bedroom, her own kitchen and her own lounge. It was a house within a house. She was eighty-five years old and fiercely **independent**. She **insisted** on making her own cold porridge, dressing herself and doing her laundry. She would not take help despite being quite **frail** and needing a walking stick. When Kiki was a **toddler**, she affectionately called her "Nanny Stick" and, since then, so has everyone else!

Kiki often asked Nanny Stick if she wanted a cup of tea or a biscuit. But the reply was always the same: "No, thank you. I can do that myself!!" Nanny was a wonderful character. She had the usual grey hair you would expect all nannies to have. Each night, she wore **curlers** in her hair to bed. Each morning, she removed the curlers, and **spritzed** on hairspray. Then she brushed and combed the curls until her locks become a **bouffant** of **hilariousness**. Kiki tried her very best not to laugh at this. But it didn't always work.

Nanny wore lipstick every single day – even though, these days, she rarely went out. The lipstick was always purple. Nanny Stick loved purple. It was her favourite colour. Nearly every jumper she ever wore was purple. She even wore purple shoes, if she could find any to fit her tiny feet. Sometimes, though, she chose lilac or **mulberry** jumpers, but she always matched.

Kiki loved living close to Nanny Stick and spent time with her every morning before she went to school. Nanny Stick was a wonderful storyteller – it was almost as if she was reading from a book. They would sit cosily on the sofa, snuggled up with tea, biscuits and sometimes a blanket whilst Nanny told her magical tales. Kiki loved to listen to them, even though they often sounded similar.

Kiki was nine years old. Her clothing **preference** was a dress of some description teamed with white ankle socks and trainers. Kiki liked comfort. She liked to be free enough to run, skip and jump and insisted that her mother always buy her comfortable and sensible shoes. She went to a small school about fifteen miles from Cravendale Cottage. It was a long journey, but her mother drove her there and back every day.

Kiki had lots of friends at school, but she knew deep down that her very best friend was Nanny Stick. It was her she told her secrets to. And it was her she wanted to spend time with. However, Nanny Stick was not as **spritely** as she once was, and as the years went by, she could no longer play with Kiki like she used to. That's why, these days, she **regaled** her with tales of adventure instead.

Nanny Stick told Kiki that Cravendale Cottage was a magical place and that, one day, Kiki would discover the magic for herself. Of course, Kiki didn't believe a word of this. She knew Nanny Stick was old, stubborn and forgetful. She knew forgetting things sometimes happens when you are really old. But she lapped up her stories as a cat would lap up cream.

Nanny Stick insisted that a magical lavender maze lay hidden in the fields behind Cravendale Cottage. "It's a family secret," she whispered to Kiki, "passed down through generations, but only to those who really believed in it." The maze was only **accessible** to those who had wisdom in their hearts and fire in their bellies, and only to those who were **inquisitive** enough to find it.

Kiki *was* inquisitive and had asked many

times how to get to the maze. Nanny Stick had given her precise instructions: "You leave the main pathway of the house and follow the **bridal path** to the end of the garden. You will see a **Monkey Puzzle tree**, which you must circle twice, remembering to stay completely silent. Legend has it that it is very unlucky to talk if you are near a Monkey Puzzle tree.

"Once you have circled the tree twice, you will see an old brick wall. It's crumbling slightly. Well, it was crumbling when *I* was a child. Many years have passed since then, so I would imagine it's almost **derelict** now. When you see the crumbling wall, you must place both hands on it and shout very loudly: LAVENDER! LAVENDER! LAVENDER!

Then the pathway will open."

Kiki had, of course, tried this several times. She had followed the bridal path to the end of the garden, but she had never once seen a Monkey Puzzle tree. She knew that Nanny Stick's stories were just stories, but secretly, in her heart, she really wanted to find that Monkey Puzzle tree.

"I had so many adventures as a child in the Lavender Maze," Nanny had told her, "and you will as well one day Kiki … but not until you really believe."

"Tell me, Nanny, what happens in the Lavender Maze?" Kiki would ask.

"It will be something different every time you enter," Nanny would reply, and then **revealed**: "For me, there was always a problem to solve; there was always someone for me to help. I didn't think I could ever do this, but the Maze would guide me, leading me to the answers.

"I met some amazing characters in that maze. It was a **labyrinth** of passages and pathways. Every time I went there, I came across a clearing, where someone was waiting …" she trailed off.

"Tell me, Nanny. Tell me some stories. Tell me!"

And they would sit for hours on the sofa whilst Nanny talked about her childhood adventures. In her heart, Kiki *so* wanted to believe the stories were real.

Chapter 2

It was a Monday morning, and the snow fell heavily on the window pane in Kiki's bedroom at Cravendale Cottage.

Kiki's room was warm. She was snuggled under her duvet, and the radiators had come on early. She could hear her mother calling her to get up. It was December, and winter had come in its full force. The snow had been falling all weekend and Kiki was hoping for a **snow day**. She was hoping school would be closed so she could pop into Nanny Stick's anncxe for tea and biscuits … and more stories. That would be SO much better than going to school.

Reluctantly, Kiki got out of bed and opened the thick-lined curtains her mum put up every winter to keep her room warmer. She looked through her window and was dazzled by the thick layer of snow. It was whiter than white, crispy and crunchy, and waiting to be played in. She did not want to go to school today.

"Kiki!" her mum yelled up the stairs.

"School is closed today, and all of the roads are blocked."

YES! YES! YES! This is exactly what she had hoped for. She **hastily** pulled on her flamingo-covered onesie and bounded down the stairs. "I am going to the annexe to see Nanny Stick, Mum. I'll be back shortly." She **exited** Cravendale Cottage through its violet front door, and entered Nanny's annex through the violet door next to it. The journey was short, but the temperature was freezing – especially as she was only wearing a onesie and slippers.

"Good morning Nan. Are you ok? Guess what? My school is closed today because the snow is falling so thick. Have you looked out of the window yet?"

Nanny Stick was at her window with an **expression** on her face of complete delight. It was almost as though her **aged** wrinkled skin had become younger. Her frown had disappeared and her tiny eyes opened widely. She was so excited she could barely speak. "Kiki, I think this is the day," she trembled.

"The day for what?" Kiki questioned.

"The very first day I discovered the Lavender Maze," Nanny replied. "I was nine years old and the snow was falling heavily, just like today. I had no school, and I went exploring in the gardens. I think today is the day *you* might find the Lavender Maze, Kiki. But you have to believe. You HAVE to believe!"

Kiki giggled. She had never really

believed in old Nanny Stick's enchanted
fairy tales. They were highly entertaining,
and she adored listening to them, but
surely, they weren't true?! They were just
fictional stories of hidden mazes, mythical
characters and amazing adventures.
"Nanny, I'm not sure I believe those
things REALLY happened," Kiki gently
responded. "But I WILL investigate. I
have a whole day off school, and I can't
wait to go out in the snow along the
bridal path to look for that Monkey
Puzzle tree."

Nanny Stick almost jumped and high-
fived her. Well, she would have jumped
and high-fived her had she not had one
hand on her walking stick and the other
hand on a sore hip. "Go, Kiki. There

is no time for tea and biscuits. There's an adventure waiting for you and a discovery to make, and I can feel it deep in my old bones."

Kiki stepped through Nanny's door, then turned towards Nanny and waved goodbye. She took four steps through the flurry of snow to her own front door, then skipped back into the house. She ran up the stairs to her bedroom and hunted for her warmest clothes. Then she charged downstairs to dig out her wellies, gloves, hat and scarf. "Mum," she called out, "I'm off to play in the garden." And before she knew it, she was stomping along the cottage pathway in snow so high it was spilling over the top of her wellies and down her legs. "Yuk," she said out loud. "My socks are squelchy!"

The falling snow was blizzard-like. It sprayed so hard on Kiki's face she could hardly see where she was going. She had thought being in the snow would be fun, but it was freezing. It was shivering cold. And it was hard work! As she entered the bridal path, the snow under her feet became uneven, making it harder to walk. She grabbed hold of bushes as she passed by them to stop herself from falling over. It was tricky to stay upright, but she was determined to make it to the spot where Nanny Stick used to see the Monkey Puzzle tree.

And then, THUD! She had tumbled over a branch that was lying on the ground and landed face down in the snow.

She hadn't hurt herself, but she could feel ice forming on her eyelashes, snow in her nostrils and mud on her cheeks. That was it; she was turning back! As she grasped the nearby tree trunk to pull herself up, she fell silent. Completely silent. Totally silent. It was here. The Monkey Puzzle tree.

Its trunk and branches towered grandly above everything else and stood **majestically** with not one flake of snow on it. Whilst everything around was covered in a blanket of white, the Monkey Puzzle tree was vibrant green. Kiki recalled Nanny explaining it was an **evergreen**, 700 years old, 160 feet tall and had once provided food for the dinosaurs. She knew not to speak, for she knew that legend said you must be silent near a Monkey Puzzle tree – otherwise, you will **invoke** bad luck.

Trembling with fear and feeling slightly **nauseous**, she searched her memory for what Nanny Stick told her to do next. "YES!" she exclaimed aloud as it came to her. "I must circle the tree TWICE." Slowly and **cautiously** she moved around the tree, careful not to touch it or make a sound. It felt like an **eternity** until she completed her second circle … and then she saw it. The crumbling wall. Just as Nanny had described! Dust filled the air. The bricks were crusty and in pieces from years of decay. In fact, it was not really a wall at all, but more a pile of **rubble** that had once been a wall.

"What next?" she asked herself silently.

21

She remembered trying to be brave and knowing that perhaps what Nanny had been telling her might be true after all. She placed both hands on the crumbling wall and, in her loudest voice, she shouted, LAVENDER! LAVENDER! LAVENDER!

Bang. Fireworks. The whole sky lit up with large **plumes** of purple smoke. It blinded her eyes and filled her nostrils. She shielded her whole face as best she could with her woollen scarf, terrified of what might happen next.

Then suddenly, it wasn't cold anymore. She became aware of the *drip! drip! drip!* of melted snow running down her skin beneath her coat collar. Next, she felt a sensation of heat on her face. **Hesitantly,** she lowered her scarf with absolutely no idea what she would see. Could it be the fallen crumbled wall still?

She blinked, blinked again, and there it was: the Lavender Maze in all its glory. Tall lavender bushes created a labyrinth maze-like form. Throughout, pathways led to the left, right, ahead and behind. The sun was gloriously high in the sky, shining so bright that Kiki continued to blink until she **acclimatised**. There was no snow to be seen. Kiki removed her coat, gloves, hat and scarf in the sweltering heat. Her welly boots and socks were too hot, too. But she needed those for walking!

She strolled to the entrance of the maze and came to a huge iron gate. It was so tall and wide it might have been made for giants. She gasped in **astonishment** as the gate creaked open. She was afraid, but she knew this was her destiny. "So Nanny Stick's stories had been true all along," Kiki thought, aware she had been entrusted with this magical family experience.

Desperate to have adventures just like Nanny had done when she was a child, Kiki knew she must walk through the gate. She remembered Nanny's words: "For me, there was always a problem to solve; there was always someone for me to help." Did someone need Kiki's help? There was only one way to find out.

Chapter 3

After walking through the gate, which was very **uneventful**, the first thing Kiki noticed was the smell. The **aroma** filled her nostrils, and she immediately felt a sense of calm. Nanny had told her that lavender can calm the **nervous system**, which would help Kiki to make important decisions. "Lavender can also make you feel better, if you are **anxious** about something," Nanny had said.

Instantly, Kiki felt a release in her body. Her shoulders, which had lifted high towards her ears, dropped down to their normal place. Her jaw and fingers, which had been clenched, released and relaxed. The smell of the Lavender Maze had acted almost like medicine. She felt calm. And all she could see for miles and miles was sunshine and lavender, which went on forever, until it met the horizon.

Cravendale Cottage was nowhere in sight, nor was the snow nor the Monkey Puzzle tree. As Kiki walked forward, she knew exactly what to expect. Every story Nanny had told her was about a clearing, and every time she visited the maze, someone needed help. Kiki continued onwards hoping to find the clearing. And as the path widened, there it was! A circle of **luscious** tall green blades cut from the maze. The lavender was all gone.

Everything was quiet except for a very slight noise. It was a huff and a puff and a grumble and a sigh. There it was again. A huff and a puff and a grumble and a sigh. And again. Huff. Puff. Grumble. Sigh. Again. Huff, Puff, Grumble, Sigh. And then, right before her eyes, a tiny **peculiar** figure appeared at the top of one of the blades of grass.

It was a little bearded man – just eight inches tall. He had a purple beard, a purple hat and coat, and red-rosy cheeks stained with tears. But who was he? And what was making him sad?

"Why are you crying, little purple man?" Kiki asked, wondering if this was who she needed to help.

"I'm purple," grumbled the man. "Purple. I'm purple! I am supposed to be GREEN!!" The man had a crazed look about him, and his huge bushy eyebrows, like a fox's tail, moved with his grumpy frown.

"Why are you supposed to be green?" asked Kiki, **genuinely** interested in the man's answer.

"I am Lucky the Leprechaun, but I guess today I am not so lucky. I should be green because leprechauns are always green. My coat should be green. My hat should be green. My shoes should be green. Most of all, my eyebrows should be green. NOT purple. A-N-D … I've lost my pot of gold," he bellowed, looking extremely cross. Kiki was speechless. She had never met a real Leprechaun before, let alone one so **cantankerous** as this one. Before she had the chance to ask more questions, he started crying again, but embarrassingly loudly this time. She put her hand up and gave his head a pat, as you would to a puppy. "It's OK, Lucky," she **empathised**. "Tell me what has happened? How on earth did you become purple? And how did you lose your pot of gold?"

"Those pesky children," began Lucky. "They set a leprechaun trap for me in my hometown … in Ireland. I am a type of fairy, you see, according to Irish folklore. I **partake** in mischief. It's part of my job as a leprechaun. I play jokes and I am a **trickster**, slightly **roguish**. And some say I cannot be trusted. They think I will **deceive** wherever possible."

He sighed, took a moment, then continued. "This is not true though. You can't tarnish every leprechaun with the same brush. I DO NOT deceive anyone and I CAN be trusted," he stated **emphatically**. "Oh, and it's my job to guard my pot of gold coins. Every leprechaun has a pot of gold coins. It's what provides us with our magic. We always hide the pot at the end of a rainbow so that no one, and I mean NO ONE, can find it …"

He is in full swing, now, and all Kiki can do is listen.

"Legend has it in Ireland that if you manage to successfully trap a leprechaun, that pot of gold will become yours. And that is what those pesky children did. They trapped me! You have no idea, Miss … Er … what is your name Miss?"

"Kiki," she replied. Then off he set again.

"Ah, you have no idea Miss Kiki how difficult it is to be a leprechaun. I have lived for hundreds of years **constantly** being chased for my pot of gold. It takes its toll on a fairy's **demeanour**, you know. I didn't think anyone would ever catch me, but here I am, trapped in this Lavender Maze and I've been turned completely purple. Huff, Puff, Grumble, Sigh."

Lucky the Leprechaun stopped talking. His cry turned into a wail and now his tears turned purple, too!

"Well, Lucky," **confided** Kiki, "I have never been to this Lavender Maze before either. My Nanny Stick used to come here all of the time as a child. She told me that it was her job to help people in the maze. She said that one day it would be my destiny too. So I wonder if, perhaps, I can help you to become green again and help you find your pot of gold."

"Can you do that, Miss Kiki?" asked Lucky. His purple tears stopped running and began to dry up.

"I have absolutely no idea, Lucky, but we can try, can't we?" she **quizzed**. "Now, first of all, I need you to tell me how the children trapped you and how you think you ended up here."

The leprechaun took a deep breath, and then he rushed out his **explanation**:

"I am a shoemaker by trade in Ireland, and we call this a '*leath bhrogan*'. I own a shoe shop, a cobbler's shop, and I make shoes for all the fairies – the good fairies, the bad fairies, the wizards and the witches.

"We leprechauns always need new shoes because we dance so much that we often make holes in the **soles**. Have you ever seen an Irish jig, Miss Kiki?"

Lucky sprang to his feet and produced a small tin instrument that he blew in to make music. He jigged and danced as he played the whistle and then stopped as quickly as he had started. "Most leprechauns are the **bankers** and the cobblers of the fairy world," he continued with his history lesson. "We are good protectors of gold and we make fabulous shoes.

"Last night, I had just finished making a pair of shoes, and I was exhausted … I had been dancing all day AND I had made a new pair of shoes for Sasha, the Snowflake Fairy, when I heard a noise coming from the human house. My cobbler shop is **located** in the garden of two young boys: they're called Ted and Fred. They are awful boys, always in trouble and forever looking for mischief. I think I panicked. I thought they were going to find my shop under the huge

toadstool and that they would get their hands on my pot of gold.

"I quickly took the pot of gold and went running across the garden. As you can see, Miss Kiki, I have very short legs so I can't run very fast. It had been a day of four seasons. We had bizarre weather: snow, rain, sunshine and wind. So I knew a rainbow was on its way, and I knew that the safest place to hide my gold was at the end of the rainbow. So I just kept running until I saw the rainbow form.

"The light of the rainbow **refracted** everywhere. Now, I know that only leprechauns can reach the end of the rainbow – and even then, sometimes there's a garden fence in the way! But I knew if I could get through the fence, and reach the end of the rainbow, I – and my pot of gold – would be safe.

"But, and **unbeknown** to me, Ted and Fred (the cheeky pair) had been **devising** a few **cunning** ideas on How to Trap a Leprechaun. They put sticky tape from one side of the fence to the other side. Now, leprechauns are short. Did I say that already? And my legs were tired from dancing. So I couldn't jump over, and I got all tangled up. My pot of gold fell to the floor and as the rainbow **rose** from the ground, everything went purple and I woke up here, without my gold!"

There was an **astonished** silence for a moment before Kiki **exclaimed**, "Goodness gracious me, what a tale Lucky. But I still don't understand how you are here in the Lavender Maze."

"Now let me think …" Lucky paused, his eyes searching skywards for help. "I think, as the rainbow rose, I got stuck in the purple colour. Rainbows are magical and no one ever really knows what happens if you accidentally get trapped in one. I was aiming for the *end* of the rainbow for safety and not for the purple colour. Now, what if Ted and Fred have taken my gold Kiki? How am I ever going to find my way out of this Lavender Maze and become green again? Huff. Puff. Grumble. Sigh."

Kiki was **perplexed**. "Lucky, I have no idea! But … perhaps if we follow the Lavender Maze, it may help us to find the answer. It may lead us back to your cobbler's shop. It may even make you green again. Come on, jump on my shoulder and let's go." She held out her hand and watched him hop on. Then she raised him up and settled him on her shoulder.

Kiki could hardly believe she was on her first Lavender Maze adventure. She had listened to so many of Nanny Stick's stories with delight. But she had never really understood the excitement of actually being there. This was *her* adventure now. Lucky needed *her* help, and she was going to do everything she could to get him back to his cobbler's shop and make him green again.

Chapter 4

The **aroma** of lavender was still as strong as when Kiki first entered the maze. But the smell kept her calm and **serene**, and reminded her of Nanny Stick.

There was lavender everywhere, and it stood tall and still because there was no breeze in the air. The lavender plants branched and spread throughout the maze with **elongated** greyish-green leaves and long flowering shoots. The leaves were covered in tiny star-shaped hairs called **trichomes** and the maze was unusual because the lavender was giant-sized. It felt safe, but Nanny Stick had warned Kiki to be careful. She remembered this as she headed out of the clearing and deeper into the maze with Lucky still **perched** on her shoulder.

They had followed the maze forward and came to their first cross path. A wall of lavender lay ahead of them so they could only turn right or left. But they had no idea which way they should go, so Lucky made the decision. "I have the luck of the Irish," he winked cheekily, as he directed

Kiki to turn left.

The heat of the sun was hot. Very hot. Kiki and Lucky felt exhausted, but they carried on and the sound of the birds singing overhead cheered them on their way.

They hadn't gone far when they stumbled on an old wishing well. Kiki and Lucky peered down inside the round shape, hoping to find some water to cool them. But it was so deep they couldn't see the bottom. It had a bucket attached to it with some thick rope. The bucket was made from dark wood, and was in a terrible condition. As they examined it, they heard a deep, bellowing voice:

"DON'T TOUCH ME!" it said, loudly.

Lucky grabbed tighter at Kiki's shoulder,

each other looking around and wondering where the voice had come from.

"Move away from me. MOVE AWAY FROM ME!" the voice instructed.

Lucky clinged tighter still and could feel Kiki trembling.

"I said … Move away from me. NOWWWWWW!!"

Suddenly, the wishing well had eyes that opened widely on the side of the aged well. The eyes and its huge eyelashes blinked, then stared straight at Lucky and Kiki.

"Don't touch me, I'm hot. Move away from me."

Kiki had never ever heard a wishing well talk. Nanny Stick had told her the Lavender Maze was magical but she

Kiki and the Lost Leprechaun

didn't remember anything about a talking wishing well – especially one with such a booming voice. She **glanced** at Lucky to see if he could reply to the wishing well, as she was unable to speak **momentarily**. Lucky, in his nervous state, resorted to dancing his Irish jig – right there, on Kiki's shoulder. It was completely **hilarious**: a talking wishing well with fluttering eyelashes and an Irish leprechaun dancing a jig. She wasn't dreaming though. She really wasn't.

"Lucky, stop it. Answer the wishing well," said Kiki.

"Ah yes, diddly diddly diddly dee ..." he sang. "How can you talk, Mr Wishing Well?"

"Everything in the Lavender Maze is

43

magical. So that's how I can talk."

Then the well turned his attention to Kiki.

"And you must be Kiki. I have been waiting for you. I am Wishy the Wishing Well. It is lovely to meet you. Nanny Stick used to visit me when she was a child. We had all sorts of wonderful **escapades**. I always hoped that one day she would send you to me. And here you are! Welcome to the Lavender Maze. How can I help you Kiki?" Wishy's **tone** had **softened**. It was kinder now. And he was offering help.

"My friend Lucky is purple because he was trapped by some awful children with sticky tape in the garden and just as the rainbow rose he got stuck in the purple colour and magically transported here," she gasped in a rush. "He is lost, so we need to help him get home to his cobbler's shop, because he needs to make some fairy shoes. He has lost his pot of gold, so until he gets it back, he has no fairy powers," Kiki **concluded** sadly.

"He lost his pot of gold? How tragic. Well there are plenty of gold coins at the bottom of my well. Do you think they might help?" asked Wishy. "They are deep, deep down, though. The only way to **access** them is to climb into my wooden bucket and lower it with the rope. What do you think?"

"Lucky, Lucky, let's do it," Kiki cried. "Let's take some of the coins from the wishing well. It can help our **quest** to return you home to Ireland."

Lucky wasn't sure. And then he became VERY sure. "You must be mad, Kiki. I am NOT going down a well in that old bucket. I know I'm called Lucky, but this is too dangerous even for me!!!"

"Lucky, if you don't do this, you may be purple forever. You may never go back to being green and you may never go home. This is a **golden opportunity**. We must get you those gold coins," said Kiki sensibly.

And so, it was decided that Lucky would **retrieve** some coins from the magical talking wishing well. Kiki looked hard at the bucket. It was ancient and **dilapidated**. It had **discoloured** from the sunlight and you could see small gaps appearing between the pieces of wood.

"This bucket is bound to leak," Kiki thought to herself. "The big question is, will it hold a leprechaun? It's a risky experiment."

Lucky jumped off Kiki's shoulder, pulling her hair slightly as he left. He landed on the edge of the bucket and quickly grabbed the rope to steady himself. With **caution**, he jumped in. He was ready for Kiki to lower the rope. Wishy had become **eerily** silent. They all focused on making sure Lucky made it safely to the bottom of the well, then back up to the top. "I hope Lucky's safe," Wishy muttered to himself. "It's been many years since anyone has tried this journey."

"Go Lucky. Go. Don't forget to collect as

many gold coins as you can. Three, Two, One!" Kiki set about lowering the bucket.

"SLOWLY! SLOWLY!" bellowed Wishy.

It took an awfully long time. "Best not to rush," Kiki thought. The rope was old and she did not want it to snap. If it did, Lucky would **plummet** deep into the murky well water. **Eventually**, she heard the tiniest splash, and she knew the bucket had reached the bottom. She could not see or hear Lucky. It was so dark down the well. But she prayed he was gathering gold coins as they had planned.

Minutes passed. She felt **tense** and panic began to set in. But then, to her enormous relief, Lucky tugged the rope, which was a sign to bring him back up.

Laboriously, she pulled the rope

upwards. The bucket felt heavy and she needed every bit of her strength until there it was: the bucket, with Lucky sitting inside on top of a heap of gold coins. They were all different sizes and shapes but they shone so brightly – almost like sunshine. They glowed so much that Kiki's eyes hurt. She covered them with her hand as Lucky screamed with delight, "Look, I have gold coins!"

A **relieved** Wishy **congratulated** Kiki and Lucky. "Well done! You now have coins to help you on your quest to return home, Lucky. I am glad I could be of help. Kiki, please send your Nanny my best regards when you see her next. Now I am exhausted. It's been an eventful morning. I'm going back to sleep!"

With that, the fluttering eyelashes closed, and Kiki and Lucky heard the sound of snoring. Quickly, they filled their pockets with gold coins. Kiki even put some in her wellies, which she was still wearing.

With the coins stuffed absolutely everywhere, they decided to move further into the maze, treading quietly at first so as not to wake Wishy. They had no idea what they would find next but guessed that the maze was **providing** them with the help they needed to return Lucky to his green colour and send him back home to Ireland to his cobbler's shop at the back of the garden.

Chapter 5

The sun was still blisteringly hot as Kiki and Lucky continued walking through the Lavender Maze. The coins they were carrying felt heavier and heavier. They had reached a crossroad but neither had a clue which way to take. They just could not decide.

The willowy giant-sized lavender was slender and graceful at each turn, and the **fragrance** hung in the **tranquil** air allowing them to **inhale** the peacefulness of the maze. Finally, they agreed to turn right and, as soon as they did, they were hit by a gigantic noise.

BUZZZZZZZ! BUZZZZZZZ! ZZZZZZ!

They put their hands over their ears and before they even realised what the noise was, they saw it: a swarm of bees circling above them. Hundreds, actually thousands, of bees. So many bees that they could hardly see. "RUN!" screamed Kiki, popping Lucky back on her shoulder. Then, struggling in her wellies filled with coins, she ran as fast as she could.

"The bees are following us," Lucky hissed in Kiki's ear. She had been stung last year at Cravendale Cottage. She was gardening with her mother and accidentally touched a bee. Its sting had pierced her **delicate** skin and she cried. She remembered her mother taking her into the house and rubbing cream into where it hurt. Kiki couldn't imagine how bad it would feel if all of these bees were to sting her and Lucky. The thought made her run faster and faster through the lavender. The ground below her was uneven. Then one of her welly boot's got caught in some bramble, taking her tumbling to the floor. Lucky grabbed onto her shoulder and fell with her.

As they looked up, the swarm of bees

formed a pattern in the sky. Kiki tried to **establish** what picture the bees were making, and then it dawned on her that it was the letter K.

The bees became silent; the queen bee flew out of the K formation and began to talk. Talking bees? "Nanny Stick never mentioned talking bees before," she thought, "but I guess if a wishing well can talk, then there is no reason why bees can't either."

"Kiki, welcome to the Lavender Maze. I am Queenie, Queen of the Bees," said the bee. "We rule here in the Lavender Maze. We gather the nectar from the lavender and **transform** it into lavender honey. The lavender is our energy source, and we have been **pollinating** this maze for hundreds of years.

"We know Nanny Stick. She is a great friend of ours and we helped her on many adventures. We hear you have a friend and are in need of our help. How can we help you?" Queenie spoke **eloquently** and softly whilst looking at Lucky, who was still on Kiki's shoulder. Feeling safe that the bees would not sting them, Kiki told Queenie all about Lucky.

"I think we can help," shrilled Queenie. "Bees, aeroplane formation please!" She spoke with such **authority** that she could have been a sergeant major and the bees her army. They followed her without question and, to Kiki and Lucky's surprise, they began to form the shape of an aeroplane above their heads. Within seconds, the plane swooped down with **impeccable precision**, picking Kiki and Lucky from the brambles and lifting them high into the sky.

The bee-plane gave Kiki an **aerial** view of the maze. It was **spectacular**. There was lavender as far as she could see, cuts in and out of the maze, left turns, right turns, roundabouts and just slightly above the maze was a purple haze. Once again, **inhaling** the **scent** gave her a sense of calm and relief. She knew the bees were there to help.

"To the honey pots," commanded Queenie and instantly the bees flew north. They flew above the maze but below the purple haze. They had begun buzzing again and Kiki's ears hurt. They flew at an alarmingly fast pace but she had a bird's eye view of the maze, albeit slightly **turbulent**.

"How on earth can a swarm of bees help me Kiki?" wailed Lucky. "I am never going to get home."

"Trust them, Lucky," she responded. "I have a feeling they know what they are doing."

After flying for what seemed like an eternity, the bees swooped back to the ground and landed. Kiki and Lucky found themselves in a wooded area full of **hives** made of wax **honeycombs**. The hive was just like a busy city ruled by Queenie herself. "My bee kingdom can help you Lucky," she said. "We can give you one of our honeypots to store your gold coins."

She gave a shrill whistle and one of her **drone bees** flew straight over. "Bring me a honeypot," she ordered. The drone bee, along with his friends, disappeared into the hive in a swarm formation and returned with a pot. There was no honey in it but it was just like the pot Lucky had used to store his gold. He was **astonished**. He could hardly believe he now had a pot of gold. He could feel his magical powers slowly returning but felt sad that he was still purple.

"Thank you, Queenie," Lucky said, "You have been so kind to me, and I am grateful to have a pot of gold."

"And I am grateful too that I no longer have to stomp around with gold coins in my wellies," laughed Kiki.

They emptied their pockets (and wellies) and filled the pot with the coins Lucky had **retrieved** from the talking wishing well. "Thank you bees," they both said and, in return, the bees swarmed into the shape of a waving hand.

Kiki and Lucky laughed as they continued on their adventure, completely unsure of what they would **encounter** next in this magical maze.

Chapter 6

Kiki, with Lucky still on her shoulder, had been walking for a long time. The soles of her feet were aching, and she was tired and **irritable**. As much as she was enjoying her adventure, she also missed Nanny Stick and longed for that feeling of comfort sitting on her sofa, drinking hot tea.

She was deep in thought when up ahead they saw the strangest sight. There were puddles everywhere. "How can there be puddles when it hasn't been raining?" she wondered. Even more bizarre, the puddles were purple – a deep shade of purple. Kiki loved puddles and she even had wellies on, so obviously she was going to jump in them.

Lucky could sense what Kiki was thinking and shrieked: "I LOVE jumping in puddles but I can't jump very high: I'm only a small leprechaun!"

"Of course you can jump, Lucky. I will teach you." Kiki took hold of Lucky in her hand and placed him gently on the ground. "Watch me," she said and immediately took off with both feet

simultaneously leaving the ground then landing in the puddle. The lavender water splashed everywhere completely **drenching** her. But she felt refreshed and cool under the mid-afternoon sun. Her laughter was loud but the sound of splashing was louder. "Come on Lucky, splash with me," she **encouraged**.

Lucky jumped into a puddle but it was the smallest little jump Kiki had ever seen. It didn't even make a splash sound and his feet hardly left the ground. "You can jump higher than that, Lucky," she said.

"No, I can't, I only have small leprechaun feet and I just can't jump high," he **retorted**.

Kiki jumped over towards him determined to help him jump higher. Of course, he could if he put his mind to it and really believed in himself. "Anything is possible, Lucky, if you try hard. Sometimes it just takes a bit of practice."

They both spent the next few hours jumping. With each jump, Lucky **gained** confidence and his jumps got higher and higher. His face was beaming with happiness as he held tightly onto his pot of gold jumping in and out of purple puddles with Kiki. They were having so much fun they didn't notice that one of the puddles was **unusually** big. In fact, it was so big it was like a small lake.

Kiki was first to jump in. She shouted at Lucky not to jump as it may be too deep for him. She picked him up and returned him to her shoulder. He shook himself like a wet dog, and she told him off for making her clothes wet. She stayed in the puddle, wading her way along. After a few steps, she saw a bridge. It was nothing extraordinary. It was just a standard bridge made of wood, and slightly rickety. She continued under the bridge and there they saw the most enchanting thing they had seen yet in the maze.

Chapter 7

Kiki blinked in astonishment. In front of her was the Lavender **Lagoon**, shimmering in all its glory. Nanny Stick had told her so much about the lagoon. The water was a deep purple colour, and lavender floated gently on top. The sky was a rich blue and not a cloud could be seen. The lagoon was really big with luscious green grass on its **perimeter**. A few of Queenie's bees buzzed overhead, but other than that it was magically quiet and still. A sight of pure beauty.

Kiki wandered over to the lagoon and lowered her hand into the purple water. It was warm, just like a bath. Before she had a chance to remove her hand she could see something under the water beginning to emerge. But she wasn't frightened, just **genuinely intrigued**. This magical maze was full of surprises. And then a head popped out of the lagoon! It was a **radiantly** beautiful lady with long purple hair in silky waves. She was the most attractive lady Kiki had ever seen.

"Hello, I am Mauve the Mermaid,"

she said by way of introduction. "It is a pleasure to meet you both. I have lived in the lagoon for many years and I know your Nanny, Kiki. I used to help her on her adventures. Do you need my help?" she asked in a well spoken, polite manner.

"Yes, yes, I do," replied Kiki. "My friend Lucky is purple and he needs to be green again so that we can send him home."

"Well, I have the perfect answer," Mauve smiled. "The lagoon **bed** is full of **phenomenal mystical** green **algae**. We, the mermaids, never go near it. We prefer to stay clean and it **wreaks havoc** on our silky hair. It turns us green for days! However, if Lucky *wants* to be green, it would be perfect for him. I can take him."

"Could you really?" asked Kiki. Lucky

had once again broken into his hilarious Irish jig and looked delighted at the prospect of drenching himself in smelly green algae. He would do whatever it took for him to get home.

"Mauve, take me to the algae, please, please," he begged. Dusk was falling on the maze and the sun was setting. And Kiki had no intention of spending the night in the maze. She knew they needed to hurry. Like Lucky, she also wanted to go home. She picked him gently from her shoulder and placed him in the mermaid's hair. He gathered two long strands in his tiny hands and used them like you would use reigns on a horse. Mauve smiled at Kiki and flew up high in the air, with her mermaid tail gracefully flipping above the lagoon. Then she dived **elegantly** head-first into the lagoon and disappeared.

Lucky gripped Mauve's hair strands tightly. He was terrified he would be separated from her as she sailed full speed underwater. She **graciously** dived deeper and deeper, and the water became darker and murkier. She slowed to a stop just above the bed of the lagoon and Lucky looked down.

The algae spread **diversely** across the floor, full of **organisms** that lacked true roots, stems or leaves – just moss-like matter. Lucky did not want to cover himself in the murky, gunky and stagnant algae that grew so densely at the bottom of the lagoon. The smell was **rancid**, but he knew that Mauve the Mermaid had

said the algae had power, so he let go of
a strand of her hair, freeing up one of
his hands.

He gathered the algae from the bed
of the lagoon and rubbed some on his
face. Then he smeared it all over himself.
He smeared it on his purple jacket, his
purple eyebrows and his purple boots.
Everything that was purple, he covered in
algae. It smelt fishy and mouldy, and the
smell was **turning** Lucky's stomach, but
he continued. Mauve the mermaid, in
her **statuesque** beauty, stared at him and
laughed. What a funny sight: a leprechaun
covered in lagoon algae.

When Lucky had finished, he took hold
of both strands of Mauve's hair again,
and she whisked him away, gliding her

mermaid tail hastily through the lagoon and back to Kiki.

Kiki had been waiting at the lagoon edge for what had seemed like an eternity. When Mauve's head appeared first, she immediately asked where Lucky was. Then Mauve flicked her tail, and Lucky went tumbling onto the luscious grass at the edge of the lagoon next to Kiki.

Kiki opened her eyes wide. She could not believe what she saw. Lucky stood in front of her, and he was GREEN! Not a mouldy, algae-smelly green but bright green, as green as the luscious grass. There was not a trace of purple on him. She couldn't believe it. Lucky couldn't believe it either. He was GREEN again!

"Thank you so much, Mauve," they both

said together. Mauve smiled, did her usual tail flick and disappeared back into the lagoon.

Lucky picked up his pot of gold and said, "Kiki, I have my pot of gold, and I am green. Now, all I need to do is get home." As he said this, they both noticed drops of water landing on them. They looked up together, and realised it was about to rain even though the sun was still shining a little bit. Dusk had nearly arrived and evening was close, meaning the sun would soon disappear.

Now, if they could just find where the sun and rain met, they would see a rainbow! Lucky could then hide his pot of gold, jump back into the green colour and go home. "Let's run, Lucky!" yelled Kiki on their **perilous** mission. "We don't have long until dusk. Run towards the sun. If the rain follows us, we will meet the rainbow."

The rain was now falling faster. Kiki picked Lucky up and returned him to her shoulder. Grateful once again for how useful her wellies had been, she ran through the maze. She was exhausted and, despite all the turns left and right, she knew they just had to follow the sun. Her legs ached and she was hungry, but she knew she had one chance to send Lucky home. Then, just as she thought her legs could carry her no further, it appeared: THE BIGGEST RAINBOW SHE HAD EVER SEEN!

And it was right in front of them.

The Lavender Maze had helped her to help Lucky. Wishy, the talking wishing well, had let them collect gold coins. Queenie, the queen bee, had given them a honey pot. Mauve, the mermaid, had let Lucky use the magical algae to turn green again. And finally, here was the rainbow.

They raced towards the green colour.

"OK, Lucky, jump! Jump like I taught you in the puddles. Jump high! Jump with confidence. You can do this!" Kiki shouted.

"Oh Kiki. I can't thank you enough. If I hadn't met you in this maze, I would have been trapped forever. I'm so grateful. I will miss you. Take care."

They hugged, and Kiki said, "OK, Lucky: One, Two, Three, JUMP!" …

The whole sky lit up green. Fireworks boomed against it, sparkling and glittering, **illuminating** the clouds.

And then … everything fell silent.

Chapter 8

Kiki was alone in the Lavender Maze now with no idea of how to get out. She yearned to return home. But she could not remember which way she had come. She and Lucky had travelled so far, and now she was here alone with **twilight looming**. Nanny Stick had never told her how to leave the maze. She had only told grand stories of entering, and her adventures. "But she never said how to get out," Kiki muttered to herself with some **irritation**.

The sun had set and she was cold. She thought of Lucky and felt happy as she had helped him return home. He was probably safe, now, in his cobbler's shop, finishing the shoes he had been making for Sasha, the Snowflake Fairy. And she was sure that Lucky would not make the mistake of being trapped again. He had probably hidden his pot of gold at the end of the rainbow where it would be safe, and he was likely telling all his leprechaun friends about the adventure he had had whilst he was lost in the Lavender Maze.

As Kiki looked around her, she began to see an imposing iron gate forming. It wasn't there before but it was being built right before her eyes. It sprung up out of the bracken, and out of the ground. It was the same gate she had opened to enter the maze! She ran as fast as she could towards the gate. It creakily opened, in need of oiling. Before she went through it, she stopped, looked back and said, "Bye Lavender Maze. I think I may be back. I think this may be the start of many adventures to come."

Then she quietly walked through the opening. The temperature on the other side was even lower than it had been that morning, and it was still snowing. She circled twice around the Monkey

Puzzle tree, remembering not to speak a word. She passed by the crumbled dusty wall. And then she trudged up the bridal path through the thick white snow back to Cravendale Cottage. She removed her wellies, feeling overwhelmed and exhausted by the events of the day. Then she opened the door to Nanny Stick's annexe. But before she could speak, Nanny Stick said, "You found the Lavender Maze didn't you, Kiki?"

"Yes, Nanny. Yes! Yes! Yes!" she replied excitedly.

"Sit down, my dear, and tell me all about it."

This time it was Kiki who told the stories and Nanny who listened.

Glossary

Access / Accessible
A place to enter or approach

Acclimatised
To get used to and adapt to new weather or new temperature

Aerial
High in the air

Aged
Got older; very old

Algae
Green water plants

Annexe
A building that is attached to or near another building

Anxious
Nervous, worried

Aroma
Smell

Astonished / Astonishment
Shocked and feeling surprised

Authority
Someone in charge, a person in command

Bankers
People who work in a bank

Beamed
To shine brightly

Bed (of the lagoon)
The bottom of the water

Bouffant
A puffed-out hair style

Bridal path
A passage used by horses (and their riders)

Cantankerous
Difficult to deal with, slightly grumpy

Caution / Cautiously
A warning, to be careful

Concluded
Finished

Confided
To trust someone with a secret

Congratulated
To say "Well done"

Constantly
Happening repeatedly

Cunning
Crafty and sly

Curlers
Things you put in your hair to make it curly

Deceive
To trick someone

Delicate
Easily broken, fragile

Demeanour
Behaviour towards others

Derelict
Empty and no longer used

Devising
Planning

Dilapidated
Old and ready to fall apart

Discoloured
Not its usual colour

Diversely
Different

Drenching
Wet, soaked

Drone bees
Male bees

Eerily
Quietly mysterious

Elegantly
Refined and graceful

Elongated
Long, lengthy, extended

Eloquently
Well-spoken

Empathised
To understand another person's feelings

Emphatically
Forcefully

Encounter
To meet someone

Encouraged
Supported; gave confidence

Escapades
Adventures

Establish
To prove something, to make firm

Eternity
Forever

Eventually
Finally, in the end

Evergreen
To have leaves all year round

Exclaimed
To speak loudly or to cry out

Exited
Left; went out from

Explanation
To have someone explain something

Expression
To say how you feel

Fragrance
Smell

Frail
Weak and easily broken

Gained
Learned, received

Generations
Family; children, parents, grandparents, great grandparents

Genuinely
Honestly

Glanced
To look

Glistened
Glittered and sparkled

Golden opportunity
An excellent chance to get something done

Graciously
To do something with grace and charm

Hastily
Quickly, fast

Havoc
To create confusion and disorder

Hesitantly
To pause and think

Hilariousness / Hilarious
Funny

Hives
A container for housing bees, a bee house

Honeycombs
Wax cells built by honeybees to store their honey

Illuminating
To light up and shine

Impeccable
Perfect

Independent
To do something alone or by yourself

Inhale / Inhaling
Breathing in

Insisted
Be very firm about
something; forceful

Intrigued
Interested and curious

Invoke
To make something
happen

Irritable / Irritation
Annoyed, cross, grumpy

Labyrinth
A maze with lots of paths
and high hedges

Lagoon
A stretch of water near a
larger body of water

Located
The location of
something; where it is

Looming
Waiting to happen

Luscious
Sweet and delicious

Majestic / Majestically
Magnificent, grand; fit for
a king or queen

Momentarily
Instantly; for a moment

Monkey Puzzle tree
A large evergreen tree

Mulberry
A dark purple colour; also
a fruit

Mystical
Full of mystery

Nauseous
To feel sick or unwell

Nervous system
A system in your body
that sends messages to
your brain

Organisms
Something having many related parts that work together as a whole

Partake
To take part in something

Peculiar
Unusual

Perched
To settle on a spot

Perilous
Dangerous and risky

Perimeter
The measurement of the outside, the whole way around the boundary

Perplexed
Puzzled and confused

Phenomenal
Extraordinary and remarkable

Picturesque
Like a picture of a painting

Plumes
Puffs of smoke

Plummet
Drop a long way quickly

Pollinating
To move pollen from plant to plant

Precision
Accurate and exactly right

Preference
To chose something you prefer

Providing
Giving something to someone

Quizzed
To question someone

Radiantly
Glowing like beams of
light

Rancid
An unpleasant smell

Ranunculi
Part of the buttercup
flower family

Ravenous
Hungry, starving

Reflected
Mirror-like

Refracted
To bounce off of
something

Regaled
To entertain and amuse

Relieved
To feel happier when a
problem is resolved

Reluctantly
To do something you
don't want to do

Retorted
To reply sharply

Retrieve / Retrieved
To bring something back

Revealed
Told an secret

Roguish
Dishonest

Rose (from the ground)
Got higher

Rubble
Rubbish; broken or
worthless things

Sash
The framework around
glass in a door or window

Scented
Has a smell

Serene
Calm and relaxed

Simultaneously
Happening at the same
time

Snow day
When the weather is too
bad to get to school

Softened
Becomes softer

Soles
The bottom of your shoes,
and the bottom of your
feet

Spectacular
Amazing

Spritely
Full of energy

Spritzed
To use a spray

Statuesque
Like a beautiful tall statue

Tense
Feeling nervous

Toadstool
A mushroom shaped plant

Toddler
A young child who has
just started to walk

Tone
The sound of your voice

Tranquil
Quiet, calm, peaceful

Transform
To change something

Trichomes
The hair structure on a
plant

Trickster
Someone who tricks
people

Turbulent
Rough

Turning (Lucky's stomach)
Made him feel unwell and a bit sick

Twilight
The time in the sky before sunset and full night-time

Unbeknown
Not known

Uneventful
Nothing important happening

Unusually
Uncommon; does not usually happen

Wreaks havoc
Causes damage

Michelle Burke

Michelle is the author of The Lavender Maze Series. She currently works as a Women's Wellness Coach at Lavender Health Ltd in Rochester, Kent. She lives with her husband, Paul, and three children. She would love to hear your reviews, so if you have enjoyed reading this book, please leave a review on Amazon.

For more information about Michelle and her books, visit: www.lavender-health.com/books

Printed in Great Britain
by Amazon

34868353R00061